SARAH'S Secret Plan

by Linda Johns
illustrated by Denise Brunkus

Troll Associates

For Theo, who came right on time
—L.J.

For Nancy, who is always ten minutes late
—D.B.

This edition published in 2001.

Printed in the United States of America.
10 9 8 7 6 5 4

Library of Congress Cataloging-in-Publication Data
Johns, Linda.
Sarah's secret plan / by Linda Johns; illustrated by Denise Brunkus.
p. cm.—
ISBN 0-8167-3693-6 (lib.) ISBN 0-8167-3512-3 (pbk.)
[1. Punctuality—Fiction. 2. Time—Fiction 3. Clocks and watches—Fiction. 4. Parent and child—Fiction.] I. Brunkus, Denise, ill. II. Title.
PZ7.J6219Sar 1995 [E]—dc20 94-39167

Sarah was waiting. Impatiently waiting.

She hoped her father would see that she was serious about getting to Ms. Wickstone's class on time.

"I'm running a little late, Sarah," her father called from upstairs. She could hear him hopping across the bedroom on one foot, trying to put a shoe on the other foot while he brushed his teeth. What he said actually sounded like "Aim gunning uh widdle ate, Ah-rah."

Sarah, of course, knew exactly how he was hopping and what he was saying. It was the same every Wednesday.

On Mondays, Tuesdays, Thursdays, and Fridays, Sarah took the bus to Amelia Earhart Elementary School. She loved taking the bus. On bus days, Sarah was always on time for school.

Wednesdays were a different story. On Wednesdays Sarah's dad dropped her off at school on his way to a weekly meeting.

"I would never miss taking my favorite daughter to school on Wednesdays," Sarah's dad always said with a chuckle.

This was her father's idea of a joke. You see, Sarah was his only daughter. In fact, she was his only child.

Sarah's mom was always late, too. "Gotta go or I'll be late for work," Sarah's mom said each morning as she ran out the door.

Sarah's parents were late for *everything*. Even on weekends. Even for fun things like going to movies.

"The movie just started," the ticket taker would say as Sarah and her parents rushed through the theater door.

"No time for popcorn," Sarah's dad would call as they hurried through the lobby and into the dark theater.

"Excuse me. Oh, so sorry!" Sarah's mom would say as they climbed over people to get to their seats.

Of course, the only seats left were always right behind tall grown-ups.

Sarah sighed as she thought about all the times she'd been late to movies. But right now it was Wednesday morning and she wished her father would hurry up and get her to school.

That night, Sarah had the most incredible idea in the history of kids. Sarah's Secret Plan would make Wednesdays run on time.

She waited until Tuesday night. Then Sarah put the Secret Plan into motion.

First, she sneaked into her parents' bedroom.

Then she crept into the bathroom...

...and back downstairs to the kitchen.

Finally, she took care of the living room when her mother was on the phone.

Sarah checked each item off her Secret Plan list.

And for the final, most convincing part of the Secret Plan, Sarah set the clock on the VCR, which for some reason always flashed "12:00."

The next day was Wednesday. Sarah's father hopped around and called down to her, "Aim gunning uh widdle ate, Ah-rah."

But Sarah wasn't worried this time. She knew her dad only thought he was late. He was actually on time, thanks to the Secret Plan.

Sarah was on time for school that Wednesday.

That weekend, Sarah's family made it to a movie *before* it started. In fact, they were early enough to get popcorn and Sarah's favorite flavor of Wild 'n' Wacky Fruit Chews.

The Secret Plan had worked! All the clocks and watches in Sarah's house were set ten minutes ahead. And now her family was always on time.

Sarah was blissfully happy—and on time—for several days.

Then things started going wrong.

"Sarah, it's time to get ready for bed," her mother said on Sunday night.

"But there are almost ten minutes left in *The Burples,*" Sarah said. *The Burples* was Sarah's favorite television show.

"My watch says it's eight o'clock, and that means it's time for bed," Sarah's mother said.

The Secret Plan Code of Super Secrecy meant Sarah couldn't tell her mother what time it really was.

Monday night Sarah's father was in the middle of a bedtime story when he glanced at his watch. "Oops. That's it for tonight," Sarah's father said as he put the book away.

Sarah didn't say anything, even though she really would have liked to hear the end of the story.

Tuesday morning, Sarah's father said, "Sarah, you'd better get out to the corner and wait for the bus now."

It was pouring rain. And the bus wouldn't arrive for another ten minutes. But Sarah couldn't say anything without revealing her Secret Plan.

That afternoon Sarah was playing with her friends Sophie and Nicole when her mother came to pick her up ten whole minutes early. "Time to go, Sarah," Sarah's mom said.

"But Mom..." said Sarah.

"Yes?" said Sarah's mother. She looked at Sarah with her eyebrows raised.

Sarah sighed. "Nothing. See you tomorrow, guys."

Sarah knew she had to do something. If she didn't act fast, she might never again see the end of *The Burples*, or hear a complete bedtime story, or finish playing a game with her friends.

It was time for Secret Plan Number 2.

That evening Sarah sneaked back into action. She worked on the clocks in the bedroom, the kitchen, the bathroom, the living room, and even her parents' watches. She set all the clocks back ten minutes. Now all the clocks in Sarah's house were set for the right time.

Sarah went to bed right on time—the right time—that night.

But then she awoke with a start in the middle of the night. She forgot to set the clock on the VCR!

Sarah rushed downstairs to the family room. And that's where she found the note.

PROGRAM
VOLUME
VOLUME
CHANNEL
CHANNEL
POWER
VHS
POWER
PLAY
Dear Sarah,
Now that you've gotten us to be on time, we've found that we actually like it. From now on we promise we'll try to be on time— especially on Wednesdays!
Love,
Mom and Dad